JAN 29 2013

FARMINGTON COMMUNTIY LIBRARY
FARMINGTON BRANCH
23500 LIBERTY STREET
FARMINGTON, MI 48335-3570
(248) 553-0300

SO-AYO-517

Stone Arch Readers are designed to provide enjoyable reading experiences, as well as opportunities to develop vocabulary, literacy skills, and comprehension. Here are a few ways to support your beginning reader:

• Talk with your child about the ideas addressed in the story.

• Discuss each illustration, mentioning the characters, where they are, and what they are doing.

• Read with expression, pointing to each word. You may want to read the whole story through and then revisit parts of the story to ensure that the meanings of words or phrases are understood.

• Talk about why the character did what he or she did and what your child would do in that situation.

• Help your child connect with characters and events in the story.

Remember, reading with your child should be fun, not forced. Each moment spent reading with your child is a priceless investment in his or her literacy life.

Gail Saunders-Smith, Ph.D.

floor section

8 × 14"

Stone Arch Readers
are published by Stone Arch Books
a Capstone Imprint
1710 Roe Crest Drive
North Mankato, Minnesota 56003
www.capstonepub.com

Copyright © 2012 by Stone Arch Books
All rights reserved. No part of this publication may be reproduced
in whole or in part, or stored in a retrieval system, or transmitted in
any form or by any means, electronic, mechanical, photocopying,
recording, or otherwise, without written permission of the publisher.

Library of Congress Cataloging-in-Publication Data
Klein, Adria F. (Adria Fay), 1947-
  Tia Tape Measure / by Adria Klein ; illustrated by Andrew Rowland.
    p. cm. — (Stone Arch readers. Tool school)
  Summary: Tia Tape Measure helps measure shelves so the new library books
can be put away.
  ISBN 978-1-4342-3046-1 (library binding)
  ISBN 978-1-4342-3388-2 (pbk.)
  [1. Measurement—Fiction. 2. Tools—Fiction. 3. Libraries—Fiction. 4. Helpfulness—
Fiction.] I. Rowland, Andrew, 1962- ill. II. Title.
  PZ7.K678324Ti 2011
  [E]—dc22   2010050219

Reading Consultants:
Gail Saunders-Smith, Ph.D.
Melinda Melton Crow, M.Ed.
Laurie K. Holland, Media Specialist

Cover Concept: Russell Griesmer
Art Director/Designer: Kay Fraser
Production Specialist: Michelle Biedscheid

Printed in the United States of America in North Mankato, Minnesota.
012012
006558R

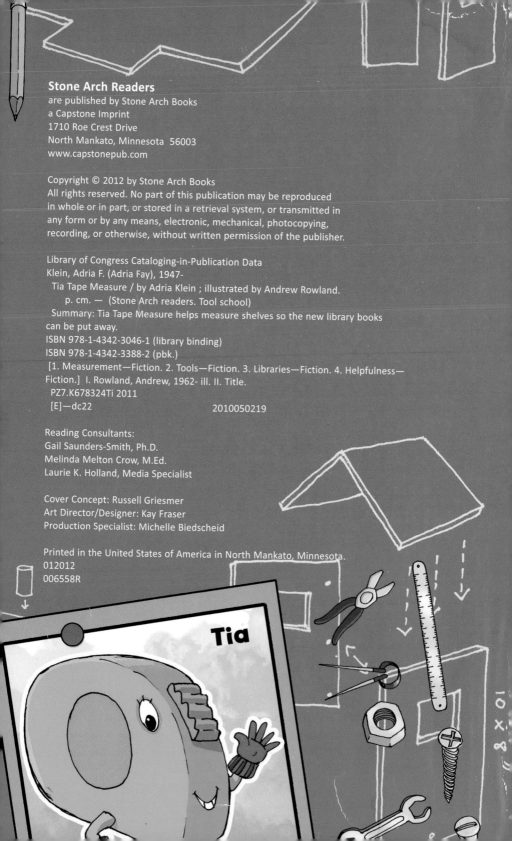

3 0036 01141 0691

Tia Tape Measure

by Adria Klein

illustrated by Andy Rowland

Sammy Saw   **Sophie Screwdriver**

"Where is Tia?" asks Sophie.

"I don't know," says Sammy.

"We can't do this job without her," says Hank.

"Here I am!" says Tia. "What's going on?"

"The library got new shelves," says Hank.

"That's great!" says Tia.

"It is. But the library is a mess," says Hank.

"How can we help?" asks Sammy.

"Follow me," says Hank.

Boxes and books were all over the library.

"This place is a mess,"
says Sophie.

"It sure is," says Hank.

"Where do we start?" asks Tia.

"First, let's put the books into piles," says Hank.

"Good idea," says Sammy.

"All the books are in piles.
Now what?" asks Tia.

"Now you need to get to work,"
says Hank.

"What should I do?" asks Tia.

"Measure everything!" says Sophie.

"No problem!" says Tia.

"Measure tall, measure small, measure twice, make it nice," says Tia.

"I need tall books for this shelf,"
she says.

"Here you go," says Hank.

"These fit great," says Tia.

"Measure tall, measure small, measure twice, make it nice," says Tia.

"I need short books for this shelf," she says.

"Here you go," says Sophie.

"These fit great," says Tia.

"We're on a roll!" says Tia.

"We sure are," says Hank.

"The library is really looking good," says Sophie.

"Good work, Tia," says Sammy.

"Thank you," says Tia. "But I couldn't do it without my friends."

"Tools rule!" they shout.

STORY WORDS

library

shelves

books

boxes

measure

twice

Total Word Count: 230

STONE ARCH READERS — LEVEL 2

TOOL SCHOOL

Sophie Screwdriver

Sammy Saw

Hank Hammer

TOOL SCHOOL